Here
The Dot We Call Home

Laura Alary

Illustrated by Cathrin Peterslund

PARACLETE PRESS
BREWSTER, MASSACHUSETTS

This is my home.
I live here.

But I am not the first.

There were people here before me.
They left some things behind.

Some were good.

Others were not.

My home has many special places.

Some are secret,
   like the hollow spot
      in the hedge,

the patch of wild strawberries
by the fence,

my calm space

in the closet

under the stairs.

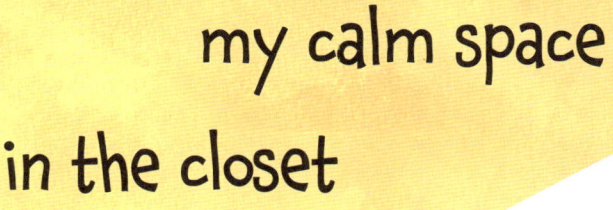

Some I share,
   like the vegetable garden
      I planted with Grandpa,

                              or our kitchen table.

As strange as it seems,
someday someone else will live here.
Will they look after my special places?

This is my home too.
                I live here.

But I am not the first.
                There were people here before me.

Before that.

Others were not.

This is my home too.

But they are still beautiful—all by themselves.
Someday other people will live here.
Will these be special places for them too?

From out here home looks so small.
How can something so big seem so small?
How can something so small seem so big?

I love my home.

I wish I could wrap my arms around it.
Care for it all.
Clean it up.
But it is too big.
And I am so small.

And this.

And this.

I can look after this.

And this.

And this.

So that is what I will do.

Start here.

2022 First Printing

Here: The Dot We Call Home

Copyright © 2022 by Laura Alary

ISBN 978-1-64060-748-4

The Paraclete Press name and logo (dove on cross) are trademarks of Paraclete Press

Library of Congress Cataloging-in-Publication Data

Names: Alary, Laura, author.
Title: Here / the dot we call home / Laura Alary.
Description: Brewster, Massachusetts : Paraclete Press, 2022. | Audience: Ages 6 | Summary: "This delightfully illustrated children's book explains that even our home has a before and after and that we need to take care of the world around us"-- Provided by publisher.
Identifiers: LCCN 2022000853 (print) | LCCN 2022000854 (ebook) | ISBN 9781640607484 (trade paperback) | ISBN 9781640607491 (epub) | ISBN 9781640607507 (pdf)
Subjects: LCSH: Home--Juvenile literature. | Human ecology--Juvenile literature. | Environmental responsibility--Juvenile literature.
Classification: LCC GT2420 .A53 2022 (print) | LCC GT2420 (ebook) | DDC 392.3/6--dc23/eng/20220207
LC record available at https://lccn.loc.gov/2022000853
LC ebook record available at https://lccn.loc.gov/2022000854

10 9 8 7 6 5 4 3 2 1

All rights reserved. No portion of this book may be reproduced, stored in an electronic retrieval system, or transmitted in any form or by any means—electronic, mechanical, photocopy, recording, or any other—except for brief quotations in printed reviews, without the prior permission of the publisher.

Published by Paraclete Press
Brewster, Massachusetts
www.paracletepress.com

Manufactured by PRINPIA Co., Ltd.
54, Gasanro 9-Gil, Geumcheon-gu, Seoul 08513, Korea
Printed in April 2022, Seoul, South Korea.